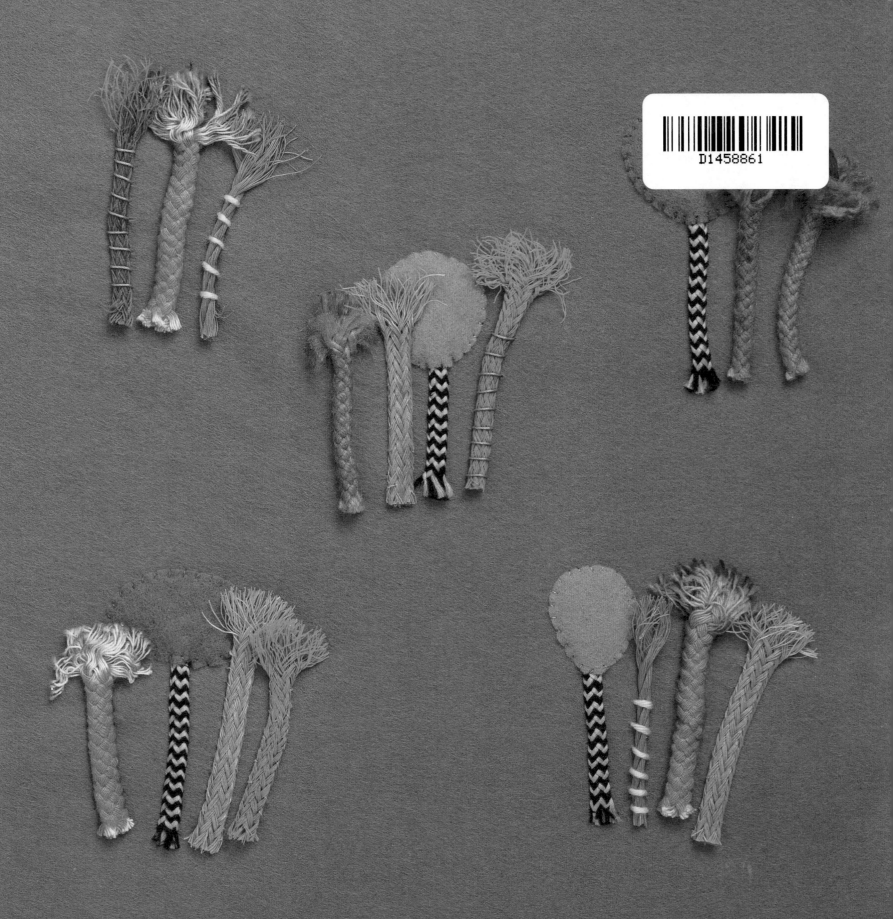

D1458861

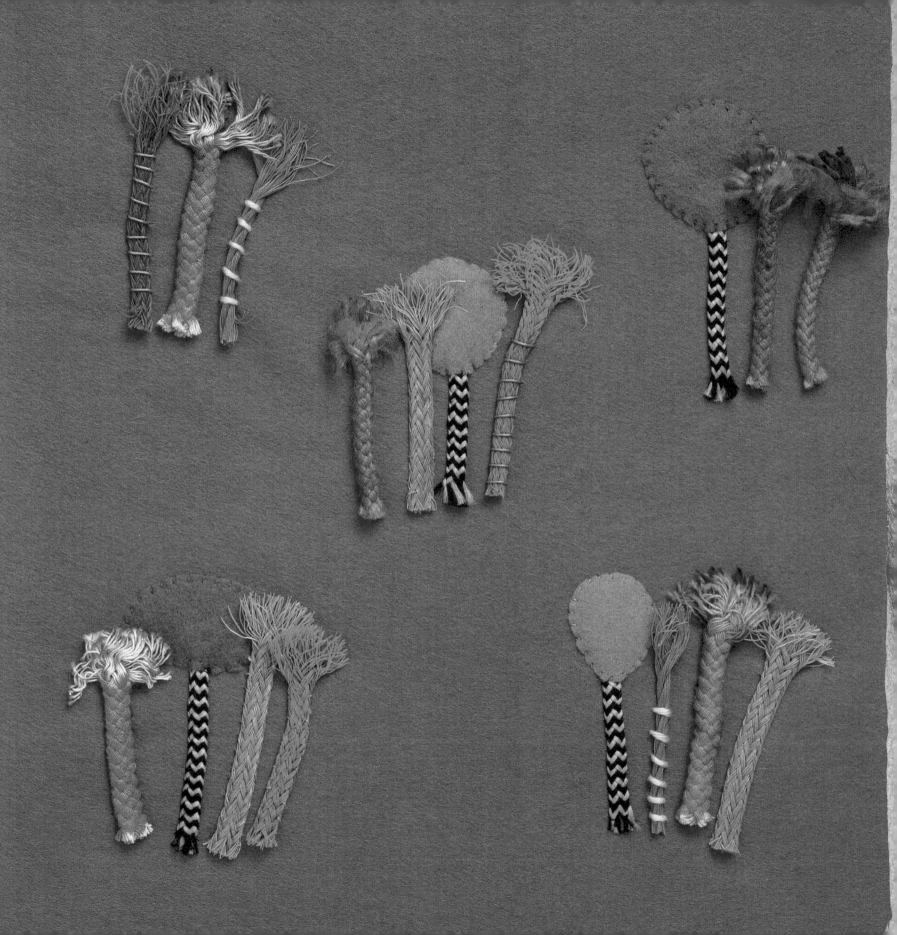

I Dreamt I Was A Dinosaur

For Carole, with thanks and love — S. B.
For Alice Jessie Jenkins, with love — C. B.

Barefoot Books
124 Walcot Street
Bath BA1 5BG

Text copyright © 2005 by Stella Blackstone. Illustrations copyright © 2005 by Clare Beaton
The moral right of Stella Blackstone to be identified as the author and Clare Beaton
to be identified as the illustrator of this work has been asserted

First published in Great Britain in 2005 by Barefoot Books, Ltd
All rights reserved. No part of this book may be reproduced in any form or by any means,
electronic or mechanical, including photocopying, recording or by any information storage
and retrieval system, without permission in writing from the publisher

This book was typeset in 21 on 28 point Bob & Eddie Bounce Light. The illustrations were prepared in
antique fabrics and felt with sequins, buttons, beads and assorted bric-a-brac

Graphic design by Judy Linard, London
Colour transparencies by Jonathan Fisher Photography, Bath
Colour separation by Bright Arts, Singapore
Printed and bound in China by South China Printing Co. Ltd

This book has been printed on 100% acid-free paper

Hardback ISBN 1-84148-237-4

British Cataloguing-in-Publication Data:
a catalogue record for this book is available from the British Library

1 3 5 7 9 8 6 4 2

I Dreamt I Was A Dinosaur

Written by **Stella Blackstone**

Illustrated by **Clare Beaton**

This book was supplied by
Moira Lumby
(Stallholder Code: UK-1000094
Tel:- 01821 640519
Email:- Moira.lumby@bellingram.co.uk
For orders or further information

Barefoot Books
Celebrating Art and Story

I dreamt I was a dinosaur.
You should have seen me romp and roar!

All kinds of creatures lived with me.
Do you want to meet them? Come and see!

Here is Sammy Stegosaurus
Busy foraging for food.

He likes Kay Camarasaurus,
But she's in a grumpy mood.

Jon and Jess Triceratops
Have a baby boy called Jed.

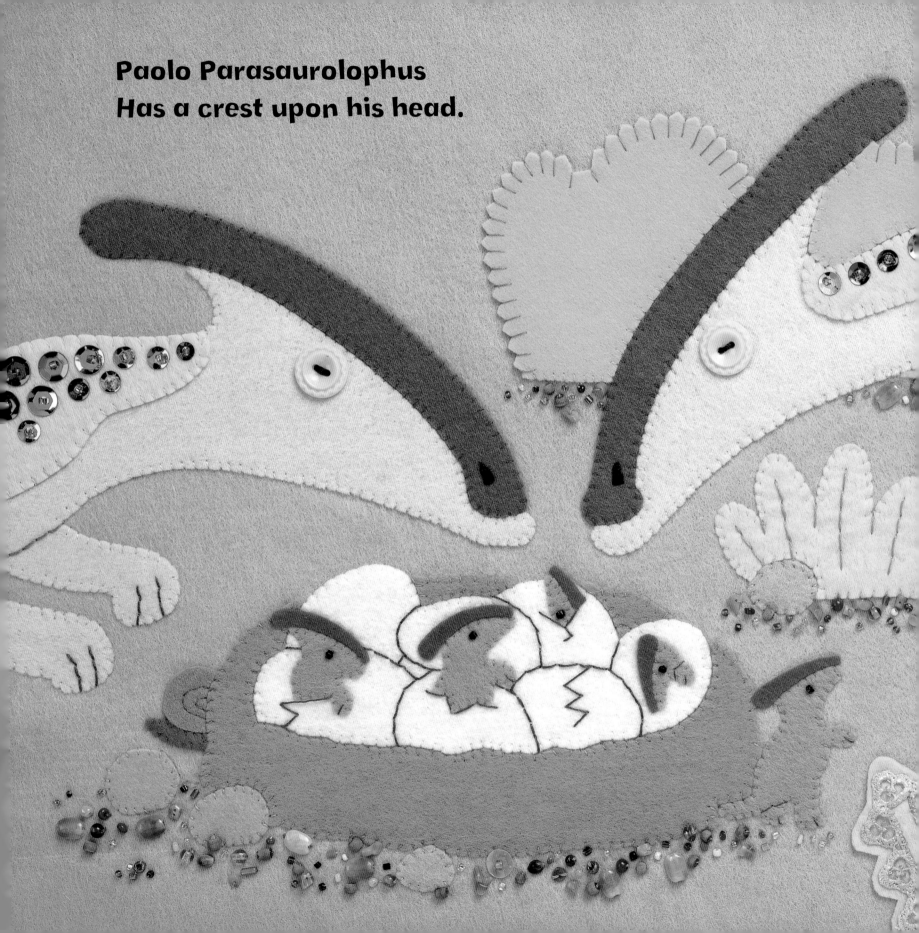

Paolo Parasaurolophus
Has a crest upon his head.

Here comes Toby Pterodactyl!
I wish I could fly like him.

And have you met Hilary Hadrosaur?
She is teaching me to swim.

I dreamt I was a dinosaur.
My life was lots of fun.

But when Rex the Wrecker came my way . . .

You should have seen me turn and run!

Then everybody disappeared — the dinosaurs had fled.
Just my baby diplodocus lay beside me in my bed.

The Age of the Dinosaurs

The word 'dinosaur' means 'terrible lizard'. Dinosaurs lived on the earth for millions of years, millions of years ago. So, no one has ever actually seen a dinosaur!

No one knows why dinosaurs disappeared, but some scientists believe that a meteorite hit the earth or that a huge volcano erupted and destroyed them.

Dinosaurs came in many different shapes and sizes. Some were massive, but others were no bigger than chickens. Some were fierce meat-eaters, while others were peaceful plant-eaters.

Some of the insects, fishes and other creatures which lived in the age of the dinosaurs are still alive now. These include birds, reptiles, turtles, dragonflies — which were much bigger than they are today — and snails, like the one that is hiding in the pages of this book.

The first people to realise they had discovered evidence of dinosaurs were Gideon and Mary Mantell in England in 1822. The Mantells dug up the fossil of an enormous creature that became known as an iguanodon. This find excited other scientists and started a worldwide dinosaur hunt, which is still going on today.

Fossils are bones and teeth that have been turned into stone over thousands of years. Since the first dinosaur was discovered, many more have been found — in deserts, on mountains and in swamps. By piecing together their fossils, scientists can work out what dinosaurs might have looked like and how they lived. No one can be sure what colours they were or how they behaved, but we do know that, like today's lizards, they had scaly skin and laid eggs.

Many dinosaur fossils have been found in Europe, North America and China. You can see reproductions of their skeletons, as well as dinosaur models, in some of the world's most famous museums. Perhaps, like the little boy in this story, you will also see them in your dreams!

Travel Back in Time!

So far, many different kinds of dinosaurs and other prehistoric creatures have been discovered, and scientists will probably find more in the future. These are the creatures that you can see in this book:

Ankylosaurus (an-ki-loh-sore-us)
Ankylosauruses were big, tank-like dinosaurs with heavily armoured bodies and club-like tails. They ate low-lying plants such as mosses, ferns and shrubby conifers.

Camarasaurus (kam-ah-rah-sore-us)
Camarasauruses were plant-eating dinosaurs. They had especially sharp teeth to chew tough leaves and twigs. They moved around slowly on their huge, pillar-like legs.

Deinonychus (day-non-ee-kus)
These meat-eating dinosaurs were lightly built, with sharp teeth, powerful jaws and keen eyes. They hunted in packs to increase their safety and strength.

Dimetrodon (die-met-roh-don)
Dimetrodons were reptiles, rather than dinosaurs. They were about 3.5 metres long and were meat-eaters. They had spiny fans on their backs and powerful jaws, with two kinds of teeth.

Diplodocus (dip-loh-doe-kus)
Diplodocuses were the largest of all the dinosaurs. These peaceful plant-eaters had small heads and very long necks that could reach the tops of trees. They used their long tails to lash out at any dinosaurs that might attack them.

Hadrosaur (had-roh-sore)
Hadrosaurs moved in herds like today's wildebeest or antelope. Some scientists think that they could swim as well as move on land. They had distinctive crests on their heads.

Omeisaurus (o-may-sore-us)
Omeisauruses were very big, plant-eating dinosaurs. They were about 20 metres long.

Parasaurolophus (pa-ra-sore-uh-low-fus)
Parasaurolophuses were plant-eating dinosaurs that looked a bit like large kangaroos. They had amazing crests on their heads, which scientists think may have made noises.

Pterodactyl (ter-oh-dak-til)
Pterodactyls were flying reptiles rather than dinosaurs and lived on insects. Some were the size of birds, while others were the size of aeroplanes.

Stegosaurus (steg-oh-sore-us)
Stegosauruses had a row of plates along their back, which probably helped them to keep cool in hot weather and warm in cold weather. They were plant-eating dinosaurs and protected themselves with their strong, spiky tails.

Struthiomimus (strooth-ee-oh-mee-mus)
These small, ostrich-like dinosaurs were meat-eaters that probably laid eggs and ran around in herds. They had toothless, bony beaks and curved claws.

Triceratops (tri-ser-ah-tops)
Triceratops were rather like rhinoceri. They had three horns and frills around their necks to protect themselves. Their parrot-like beaks helped to tear the tough plants they ate.

Tyrannosaurus Rex (tie-ran-oh-sore-us rex)
These were the biggest and fiercest of the meat-eating dinosaurs, with huge jaws and sharp teeth. They probably could not move very fast, because they were so huge, and they walked upright on their hind legs.

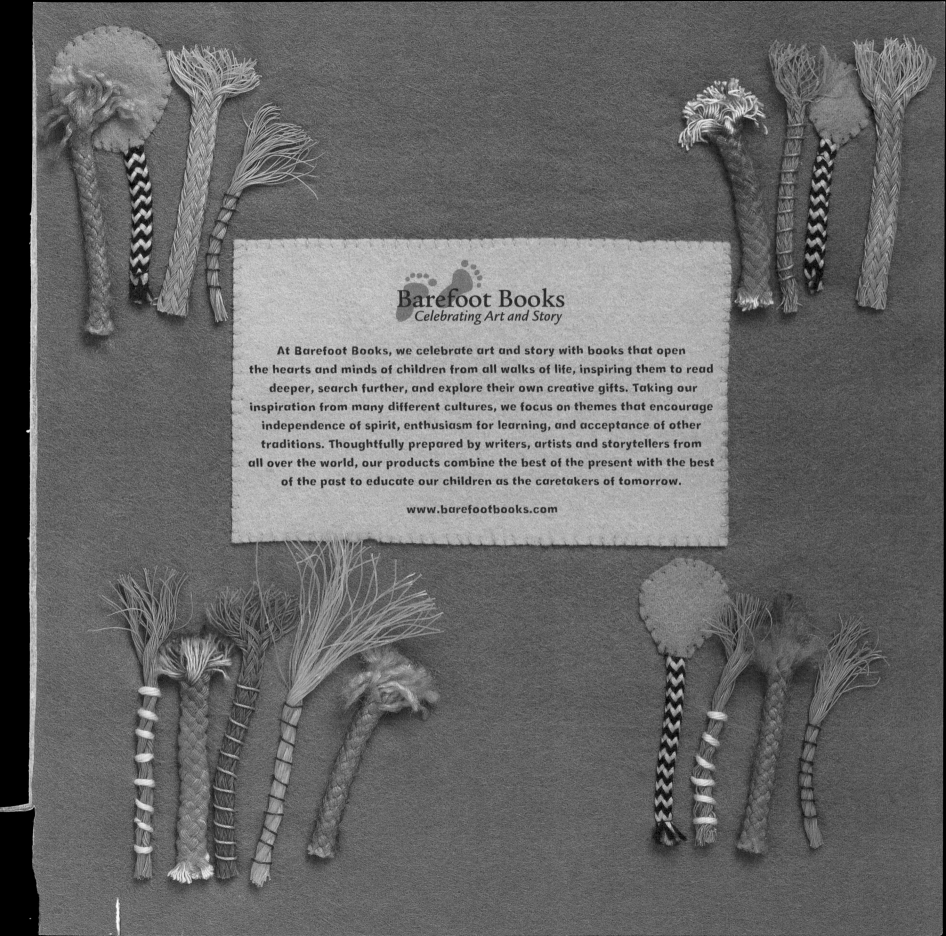

Barefoot Books
Celebrating Art and Story

At Barefoot Books, we celebrate art and story with books that open the hearts and minds of children from all walks of life, inspiring them to read deeper, search further, and explore their own creative gifts. Taking our inspiration from many different cultures, we focus on themes that encourage independence of spirit, enthusiasm for learning, and acceptance of other traditions. Thoughtfully prepared by writers, artists and storytellers from all over the world, our products combine the best of the present with the best of the past to educate our children as the caretakers of tomorrow.

www.barefootbooks.com

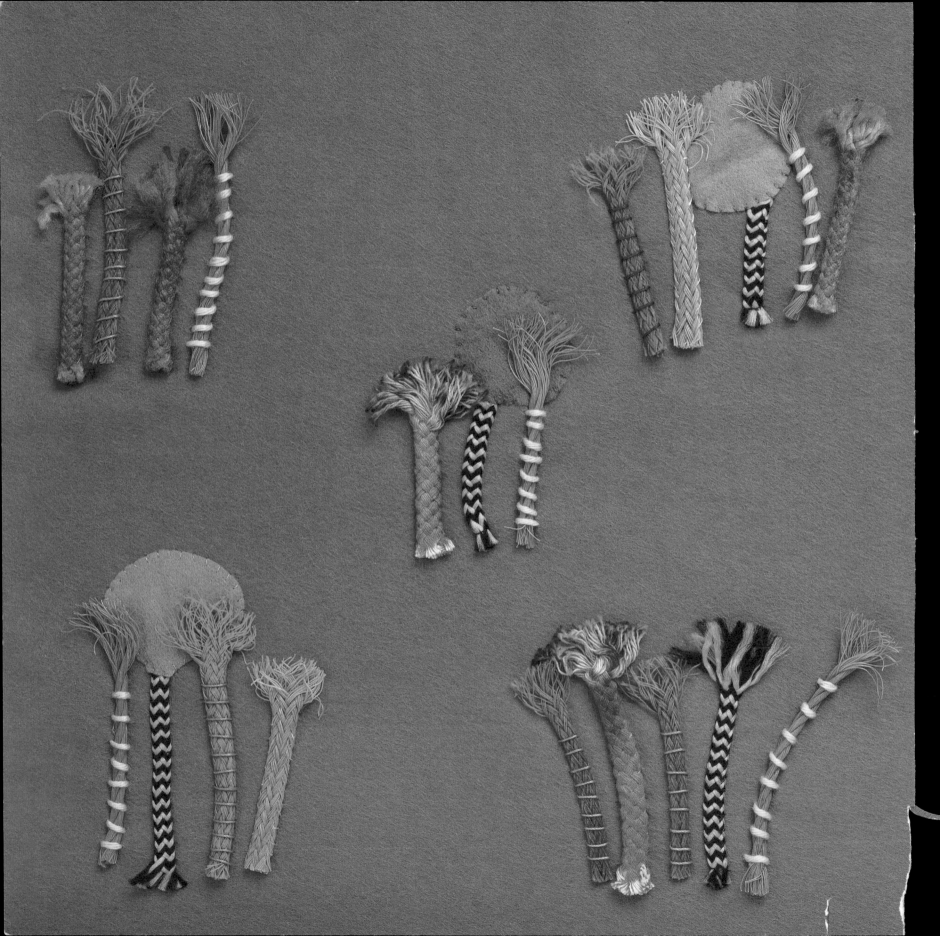